Maguy et David
Katy et Robert

Papa
et
Maman

my love

Jadyn
and the
Magic Bubble

Jadyn and the Magic Bubble
Discovering India

Copyright © 2007 by Brigitte Benchimol

Published by:
East West Discovery Press
P.O. Box 2393, Gardena, CA 90247
Phone: 310-532-1115, Fax: 310-768-8926
Website: www.eastwestdiscovery.com

Author: Brigitte Benchimol
Editor: Jennifer Thomas-Hollenbeck
Co-Illustrator: Siegfried Zima
Book design and production: Brigitte Benchimol and Jennifer Thomas-Hollenbeck

Library of Congress Cataloging-in-Publication Data

Benchimol, Brigitte, 1963-
   Jadyn and the magic bubble : discovering India / by Brigitte Benchimol. -- 1st U.S. ed.
      p. cm.
   Summary: Jadyn visits India with the help of some magic bubbles and learns about its culture and history. Includes activities, recipe, facts about India, and musical CD.
   ISBN-13: 978-0-9701654-9-7 (hardcover : alk. paper) [1. India--Fiction.] I. Title.
   PZ7.B4311Jad 2007
   [E]--dc22

                                    2006028671

ISBN-10: 0-9701654-9-8, hardcover with CD
ISBN-13: 978-0-9701654-9-7, hardcover with CD

First U.S. edition 2007
Published in the United States of America
Printed in China

Jadyn and the Magic Bubble

Discovering India

by
Brigitte Benchimol

East West Discovery Press

The school bell rang. I threw my books in my backpack,
said goodbye to my teacher, and ran outside
and jumped on my bicycle,
like Batman into the Batmobile.

"Bye, Jadyn!" yelled my friends. "Are you coming to
Timmy's birthday party tomorrow?"

"I can't!" I yelled back. "I have to write my report about
a famous foreign personality who changed the world.
Have a good weekend! Bye!"

This assignment was due Tuesday
and I hadn't yet decided whom to choose.
But I would figure it out soon.

I stopped at the library to get some books
about different foreign personalities.
Nicki, the librarian, helped me find them.

Books are my best friends:
I can take them everywhere and imagine anything.

Afterward, I jumped back on my bicycle
and sped up to get home fast.

I said hello to my mom
and climbed the stairs to my bedroom,
like Robin Hood, dodging arrows as I went.

I put my books on my desk,
noticing that the one on top was about "Gandhi,"
a peculiar-looking man with round glasses.

I didn't know who Gandhi was,
but I would have plenty of time to read about him
over the weekend.

I sat on my bed and noticed a small present sitting there.
An itsy-bitsy card was attached to it:

My sweet Jadyn,
A little gift that will blow your mind!
And remember:
Life is a journey, not a destination.
Love forever,
your Aunt Leah

Aunt Leah always gave me
the most interesting gifts with secret messages.

I unwrapped the paper and inside was
a colorful bottle with a label that read:

MAGIC BUBBLES: Not for everyone!

Now I was really intrigued.

I started to blow my new magic bubbles.

The bubbles were all different colors—
rainbow colors, transparent and opaque.
I wanted to hold them before they vanished.

As I got close, I noticed a strange bubble
with a whole other world in it—
different colors and people in motion.

It was so bizarre! So full of life!
I had never seen anything like it before.

Suddenly the bubble burst and…

Whoaaaaaaaaaaa!!!!!

It swallowed me.

In a flash, I was surrounded by a strange new world.

I was in a large street, overflowing
with people and animals everywhere.
Some of the people didn't even have shoes,
and others were rushing about on strange bikes,
carting people.

Different smells, loud noises, and honking cars.

On a street corner,
a little shoeless girl was begging for money.
Our eyes met, but I quickly turned my head the other way.
It hurt to look at her: she looked so poor, so thin.
Her little face engraved itself in my mind.

Out of the blue, a boy about my age appeared!

"Welcome to New Delhi, my friend!"

"New Delhi? The New Delhi in India?"
I was puzzled and scared at the same time.

"Very good. New Delhi is the capital of India, and
it should be here for a few thousand more years, I hope!"
The boy laughed with a big wide smile.

All around me were people,
some living in poverty and some in wealth.
Poverty frightened me.
I had never seen anything like that before.

"I'm Anil. What's your name?"
"Jadyn."

"Let me show you how people in India live, my friend."

Anil saw me looking like a deer in the headlights.
"Don't worry, Jadyn; you'll be safe with me.
You'll like India. Everybody does."

Anil didn't seem to be poor or sick
like some of the people around me.
He even wore shoes.
"All right, I'll go with you."

17

We became friends immediately.
Anil had straight charcoal hair and
a face the color of topaz.

"Let's go! I'm going to show you everything about
this city," he said proudly, grabbing my arm.

"But first," he said, "I would like to take you
to Agra to show you the Taj Mahal."

I had no idea about Agra or the Taj Mahal,
but I agreed to go with him.
We jumped in a cab and headed to Agra.

On our long trip, Anil told me all about India.
He said that the Taj Mahal was on the
banks of the Yamuna river.
I couldn't wait to see it!

"Look, Jadyn!

LOOOOOOOOK...

This is the Taj Mahal."

"Whoa, it's A-MA-ZING!"

"You're right, my friend. It *is* A-MA-ZING!
You know why it's here?"

"No, but you do." My curiosity was piqued.

"Of course I do. The Taj Mahal is one of the
Seven Wonders of the World.
It's here because of...LOVE."

"Love? What does love have to do with it?"

"AAAAAh, LOVE!" he sighed.
"Emperor Shah Jahan had a wife
named Mumtaz Mahal whom he loved eternally.
When she died, the Emperor was heartbroken.
So he built the most beautiful monument in her honor:
he built the Taj Mahal because he loved her so much.
Both the Emperor's and his wife's tombs
are inside this mausoleum."

The noise of street hawkers and car horns
drew me out of my daydream.

"Welcome back to New Delhi!" said Anil.

We alighted from the cab and started walking.

As we made our way down a narrow side street,
a small woman busily working attracted my attention.
She was in a dark alley,
but despite the poverty she was full of joy.

"What is she doing?" I asked.

"Jadyn, my friend, do you know how we make silk?"

"No, I don't."

"Let's go and the silk lady will show you!"

As we approached the woman in her shop,
she looked up at us and said:

"You boys are curious about silk, aren't you?
That's very good. Knowledge is power.
I'm Uma.
Instead of telling you the story
of how to make silk,
I'm going to sing it to you:

"The worm wraps himself in his cocoon;
I'll pull the threads from the cocoon.
Thank you, worm, for the nice gift,
Offering us your so, so soft silk."

"Bravo, bravo!" I shouted, clapping my hands.

Uma sang like a bird and worked like a bee.
She came to me with the long thin piece of orange silk
she had just created before my eyes
and wrapped it around my neck like a scarf.

"Here, Jadyn, this is my welcome gift to you.
India is a wonderful country.
Sometimes we may be disturbed
by what we see around us,
but it is from all of our feelings that we grow."

I hugged Uma to thank her for her kindness.
I told her I would remember how to make silk, forever.

As we walked away, I noticed a sign over Uma's door:

We must be the change we wish to see in the world.
~Mahatma Gandhi (1869-1948)

This quote intrigued me;
it was by the man from the book
I had borrowed from the library:
Mahatma Gandhi.

"Come on, my friend.
We have more things to do in New Delhi.
Let's go!"

Anil stopped one of those funny tricycles.
It had three wheels and a little carriage in the back
to transport people or packages.

A thin but strong older man was pedaling fast
but stopped as soon as Anil waved at him.

"What are these funny vehicles?" I asked.

"Long ago, rickshaws were the only means of
transportation throughout the cities of India.
But now, they have mostly been replaced
by auto rickshaws," said Anil.
"You are really lucky we have spotted one today.
So let's enjoy the ride!"

As we passed by food stands in the street,
Anil noticed my eyes growing big.

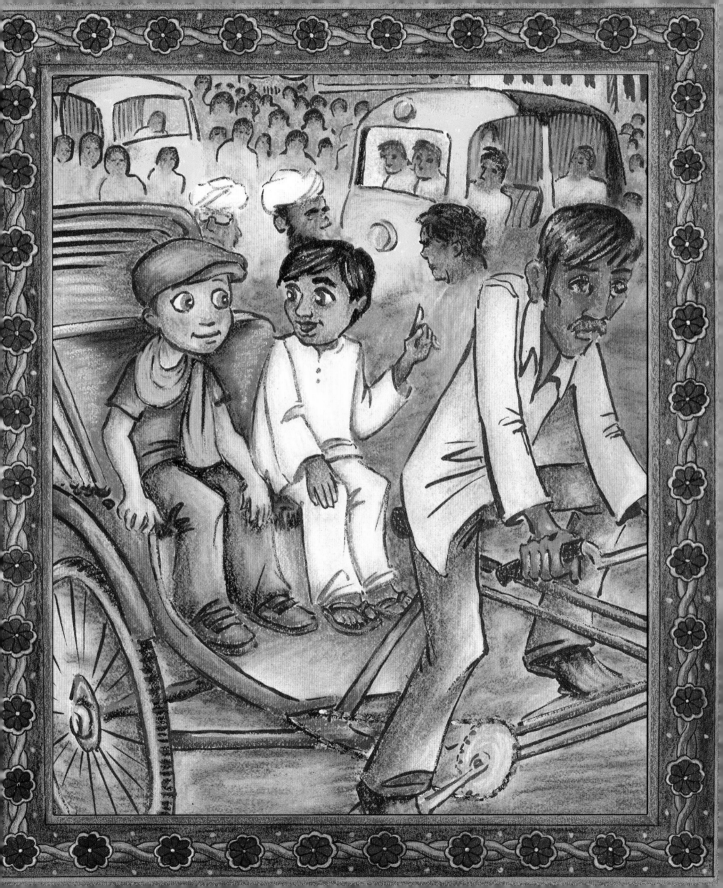

"Are you hungry?" Anil asked me.
"Ooh, yes," I replied.

I had to try the local specialties;
it was part of my discovery.

My mom and I spent a lot of time
together in the kitchen:
cooking and tasting and eating and playing and laughing.
As a result, I loved food.

Anil asked the rickshaw driver to stop.

We wandered the streets trying out all sorts of
yummy foods I had never tasted:
naan, samosas, aloo gobi.

The sights and sounds of the streets—
the different delicious aromas;
the bright exciting colors;
the harmonious blend of music playing in the street;
and the softness of the silk scarf around my neck—
tickled all of my senses.

Suddenly I noticed the little shoeless girl
looking at the food stands.
But I was too shy to approach her.
I didn't know what to say to her.

Meanwhile, Anil bought a sweet dessert
for me to taste and enjoy.
It was a kind of rice pudding,
called *kheer,* with broken pistachios in it.

"Yummmm," I said enthusiastically.
"This is the most delicious dessert I've ever had!"

"Do you have a sweet tooth?" asked Anil.
"Because I do.
I think all my teeth are sweet
and that's why I like dessert so much!!"

"I'm like you—all my teeth are sweet too!!" I replied.

We both left laughing
about all the things we had in common,
but mostly our love of desserts.

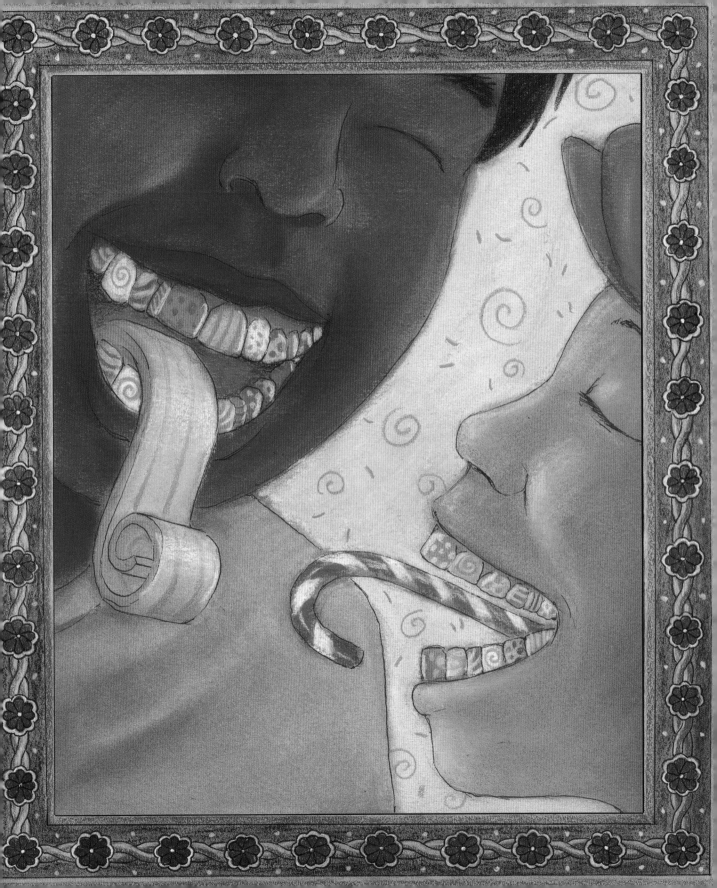

After that sweet experience,
we jumped back into the rickshaw
and went to pick up Anil's older sister at school.

Her name was Shivani.
She looked dazzling with her long ebony hair
woven in a single thick braid down to her waist.
Her skin was the color of the sun at dusk,
her eyes were like marcasite stones,
and her lips were the color of a rose.
She wore a sari of orange and purple silk.

Her beauty struck me.

"How was the ceremony at school?" asked Anil.

"It was meaningful, as always," she answered
as she climbed into the rickshaw.

"Hello! Who are you?" she asked me.

"I'm Jadyn. I'm Anil's friend."

"I have never met you before. You must be a new friend!"

As the rickshaw began to pull away,
I again noticed the little shoeless girl.
She was standing on the sidewalk waving at us.

This time, I asked the rickshaw driver to stop.

I jumped off and walked toward her.
I was nervous, really nervous.
I remembered Uma's words:
"It is from all of our feelings that we grow."
I was ready.

I stood in front of the little girl.
Her big eyes stared at me, then at the scarf.
Spontaneously, I took the scarf from around my neck
and draped it around hers.

She couldn't say a word—
she seemed so amazed and happy.

She stood on her tippy toes,
kissed me on the cheek,
and ran away.

As she disappeared into the crowd, I felt so light—
as if she had given me wings.

As I returned to our rickshaw, I noticed that
Shivani's school was named after Mahatma Gandhi.
I knew that the third time was no coincidence—
it had to be a sign.

I asked Shivani about Mahatma Gandhi.

Shivani explained to me gently:
"*Mahatma* means great soul.
His full name was Mohandas Karamchand Gandhi,
and he led the people of India to independence from the British.
He preached nonviolence and passive resistance.
He lived with the poorest people in India
to understand their suffering."

"Was he like Martin Luther King Jr., in a way?" I asked.

"Actually," replied Shivani, obviously impressed by my remark,
"Dr. King was inspired by Mahatma Gandhi."

Suddenly Shivani's words reminded me of something.

I remembered my mother explaining to me
how important Martin Luther King Jr. was.
How important it was to have dreams, to share those dreams,
and to lead other people toward realizing those dreams.
How dreams, great intentions, and hard work
can help our world to grow and get better.

I heard my mother telling me,
gazing at me with her big emerald eyes:
"Jadyn, my love, when you dream
or when you wish something with all your heart,
your wish will come true.
Life is full of magic. You are full of magic.
You just have to use it to great purpose.
I will always support you."

Then she added in a whisper:

"Never give up on your dreams."

Just then, a lonely bubble floated toward me from the sky.

The bubble had a little halo surrounding it.
It circled me a few times and wrapped around me like a sari!
I guessed it was time to go back home.

I was back in my bedroom,
still moved by my experience.
Everyone I'd met had welcomed me
and shared what they had.

Why was it so hard to leave my bedroom?
How was it possible to be curious and scared at the same time?

I thought of all my favorite heroes:
Batman and Robin, Superman and Zorro,
and I wondered if they ever felt fear.

Maybe they did.
Just because they didn't show it
didn't mean they didn't feel it.
Maybe they liked to have a little bit of fear,
just to conquer it.

In India, I'd had to conquer my fears too.
I had left the cocoon of my own bedroom and loved it.

I was still thinking about my adventure
when I heard my dad calling me from the kitchen:
"Jadyn, dinner is ready!"

I got up slowly and went down the stairs,
my nose still filled with the aroma of curry
from my sensory journey in India.

As I neared the table,
my parents each gave me a kiss
and my mom said:
"So, Jadyn, have you decided
which famous foreign personality to write about yet?"

"Well, I'm not sure, but I have an idea."

"All right. Would you like to share it with us?"

We sat down.

My dad laid some dishes on the table
and my mom told me:
"We're having fish curry with aloo gobi for dinner
and kheer for dessert tonight.
I hope you like it!"

My jaw dropped in astonishment.
This *couldn't* be just coincidence.

"I'm pretty sure I will!
Especially since I'm writing my essay on Mahatma Gandhi!"
I replied with Anil's big smile on my face.

Now it was my parents who were astonished.
They looked at each other,
then turned back to me and cheered in unison:

"Great choice, Jadyn!"

To be continued...

ACTIVITIES FOR THE SENSES

TASTE
Make the dinner that Jadyn was eating with his family (see recipes included):
- *Aloo gobi* is cauliflower and potatoes.
- *Kheer* is an Indian rice pudding.

SMELL
- Smell the delicious dishes that you have prepared with your family.
- Smell the curry.

SIGHT
- Draw and color the flag of India.
- Draw and color the map of India.
- Draw a picture of some colorful things you can see in India.

SOUND
- Listen to Jadyn's CD.
- Find more Indian music to listen to.

LANGUAGE
Learn few words of Hindi:
- Mother: *Mata*
- Father: *Pita*
- Teacher: *Guru*

TOUCH
- Touch the piece of Jadyn's silk scarf.
- Dress Indian style: Using an old sheet, experiment with wrapping a turban or a sari.

IMAGINE
What would you build for the person you love the most?
- Tell the story.
- Draw a picture.

JADYN'S QUIZ

FIND THE ANSWERS IN JADYN'S STORY

❀ What is the name of the boy who welcomes Jadyn?

❀ What is the name of the beautiful monument that Jadyn visits? Who built the monument and why?

❀ How does Uma make silk?

❀ Which dessert does Jadyn discover with Anil's help?

❀ Who was Mahatma Gandhi?

❀ Who was Martin Luther King Jr.?

❀ What is Shivani wearing?

❀ What does Jadyn's mom mean when she says: "Never give up on your dreams"?

❀ Name three precious stones mentioned in the story.

❀ Name three feelings that Jadyn shares with us.

SHIVANI'S ALOO GOBI

PREPARATION TIME 1 hour

SERVES 4–6 people

INGREDIENTS

2 big potatoes, washed, peeled, and cut into small pieces
1 stalk of cauliflower, washed and broken into small pieces
2 onions, cut into chunks (halve each onion and cut each half into 4 pieces)
3 Tbsp oil
3 Tbsp cumin seeds
3 Tbsp mustard seeds
3 Tbsp coriander powder
2 cloves of garlic, chopped
1 sprig curry leaves
1 tall glass of water
1 tsp salt to taste
Pinch of cayenne pepper, if you like it spicy *(If not, you can skip this ingredient!)*
1 sprig coriander leaves for decoration

DIRECTIONS
Make sure to have an adult help you!

- Heat oil in a large pan.
- Season oil with mustard seeds, cumin seeds, and curry leaves.
- Mix for a few minutes.
- Add onions and cook until brown.
- Add the garlic, cauliflower, and water. Cook for 10 minutes.
- Add the potatoes and coriander powder.
- Add salt and cayenne pepper to taste.
- Let the entire mixture cook until the cauliflower and potatoes soften.

You are done!

READY TO EAT?
   Don't forget to decorate by sprinkling with coriander leaves. Enjoy!

Eat with friends or family around the table and it will taste even better!
YUMMMY!!

ANIL'S SWEET KHEER

PREPARATION TIME 1 hour 15 minutes

SERVES 4–5 people

INGREDIENTS

4 handfuls white basmati rice
3 tall glasses of water
3 tall glasses of milk
4 Tbsp condensed milk
1 tsp cardamon
1½ handfuls chopped pistachios
1½ handfuls sliced almonds
1½ handfuls raisins

I always use my mother's handfuls and, like me, you always want to cook supervised by an adult!

DIRECTIONS

- Cook rice in a pan with the water.
- When the rice is cooked, drain the water and put the rice back in the pan with the milk and all the other ingredients except the saffron.
- Simmer on low heat and stir regularly.
- When the mixture reaches a semi-thick consistency and a rich, creamy color, turn off the heat. It's ready!

Be patient and enjoy the process!

READY TO EAT?

Add a personal touch to your dish
by decorating it before serving.

Be creative!

Sprinkle with saffron, broken pistachios,
or whatever else you think will enhance the look and flavor!

You can eat your kheer warm or really chilled.
YUUUUUUUMMMMMMMMMMMMMMYYYYYYYYYYYY!!!!!!

A FLAG FOR EACH COUNTRY

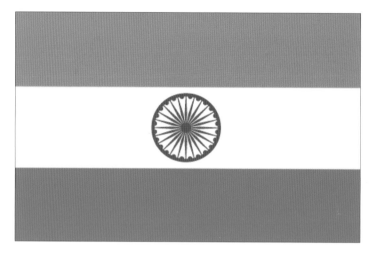

India adopted its National Flag in 1947 as the symbol of its independence.

The Indian flag is called *Tiranga,* which means *tricolor* in Hindi:
deep saffron at the top, white in the middle, and green at the bottom,
in 3 equal bands.

The spinning wheel in the center is blue with 24 spokes.

Why those colors and why the spinning wheel?
The colors were chosen with care to represent India:

The saffron stands for courage, sacrifice, and the spirit of renunciation.
The white represents purity and truth.
The green stands for faith and fertility.

The Ashoka Wheel, also called the *chakra,* represents the motion of life;
it imparts an important message:

*Everything changes and we can't resist change;
we need to embrace change, so we can move forward peacefully.*

 DRAW A FLAG OF AN IMAGINARY COUNTRY OF YOUR CHOICE.
EXPLAIN THE MEANING OF THE COLORS OR SYMBOLS YOU CHOOSE.

DID YOU KNOW?

HOW MANY PEOPLE LIVE IN INDIA?
1,095,351,995 - One billion, 95 million, 351 thousand, nine hundred ninety-five! (estimated, July 2006)

WHAT IS THE CAPITAL OF INDIA?
New Delhi.

WHAT RELIGIONS ARE PRACTICED IN INDIA?
Hinduism, Islam, Christianity, Jainism, and Buddhism are the most common.

WHAT LANGUAGES ARE SPOKEN IN INDIA?
Hindi is the national language. Bengali, Gujarati, Kannada, Kashmiri, Malayalam, Marathi, Punjabi, Sanskrit, Tamil, Telugu Urdu, and English are also official languages.

WHAT FABRIC IS PRODUCED IN INDIA?
Silk.

WHAT GARMENT DOES A TRADITIONAL INDIAN WOMAN WEAR?
A sari.

WHAT ARE THREE DISHES THAT PEOPLE EAT IN INDIA?
Aloo gobi, samosas, kheer.

WHAT IS ONE OF THE MOST BEAUTIFUL BUILDINGS IN THE WORLD, FOUND IN INDIA?
The Taj Mahal.

WHO WAS ONE OF THE MOST IMPORTANT FIGURES IN INDIA'S HISTORY?
Mahatma Gandhi, also called Mohandas Gandhi.

READY FOR MORE ADVENTURES?

Look for Jadyn's all new magic bubble adventure:
I Met Gandhi

Jadyn finally decides to write his essay on Mahatma Gandhi.
What he doesn't expect is for one of his magic bubbles to drop him back in time,
offering him the incredible chance to meet with Gandhi face to face.
Jadyn learns a lot about this man who changed the world,
and even more about himself.

Another Inside/Out Discovery

"This book is an amazingly imaginative way of bringing Gandhi's message to children. I hope all children read it and learn that peace is possible and that the children, the leaders of tomorrow, can make a difference."

—*Arun Gandhi*
President, M. K. Gandhi Institute for Nonviolence
Memphis, TN, USA